Pandora

A Greek Myth

retold by Laura Layton Strom
illustrated by Stefania Bisacco

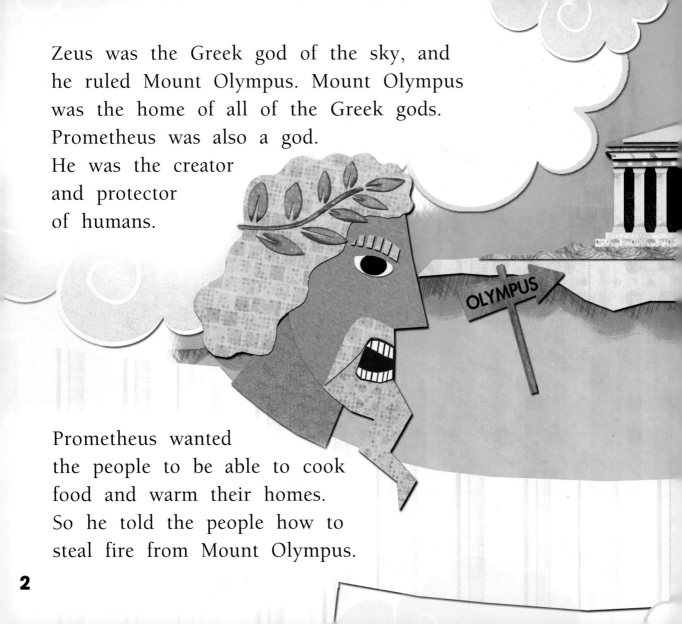

Zeus was the Greek god of the sky, and he ruled Mount Olympus. Mount Olympus was the home of all of the Greek gods. Prometheus was also a god. He was the creator and protector of humans.

Prometheus wanted the people to be able to cook food and warm their homes. So he told the people how to steal fire from Mount Olympus.

OLYMPUS

2

Zeus was very angry. "The people have their own source of fire now! They no longer need to respect the gods to receive this gift!"

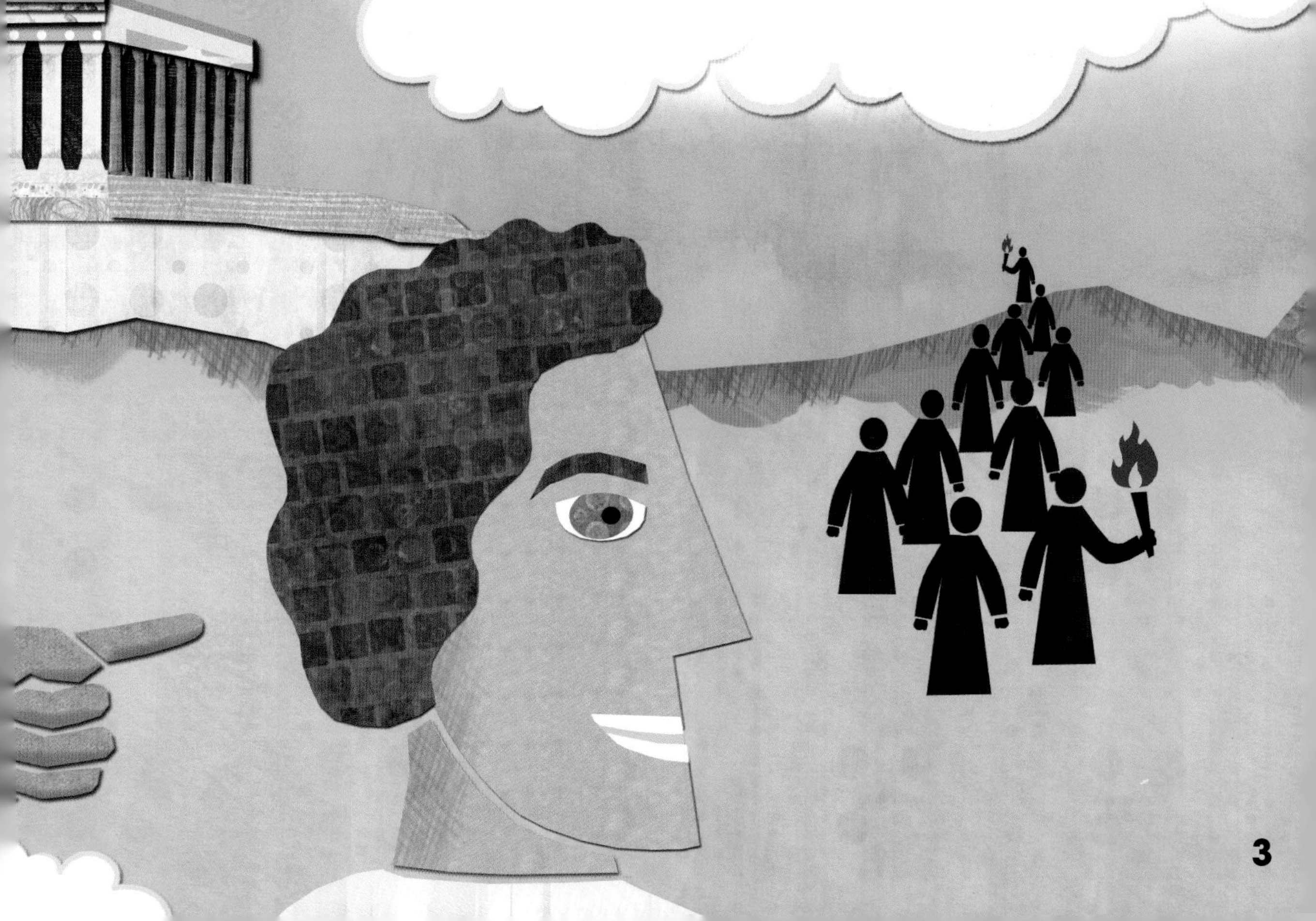

Zeus punished Prometheus, but he was angrier with the people themselves. “The people must pay for stealing from the heavens!” he raged. So Zeus came up with a plan to get back at the people.

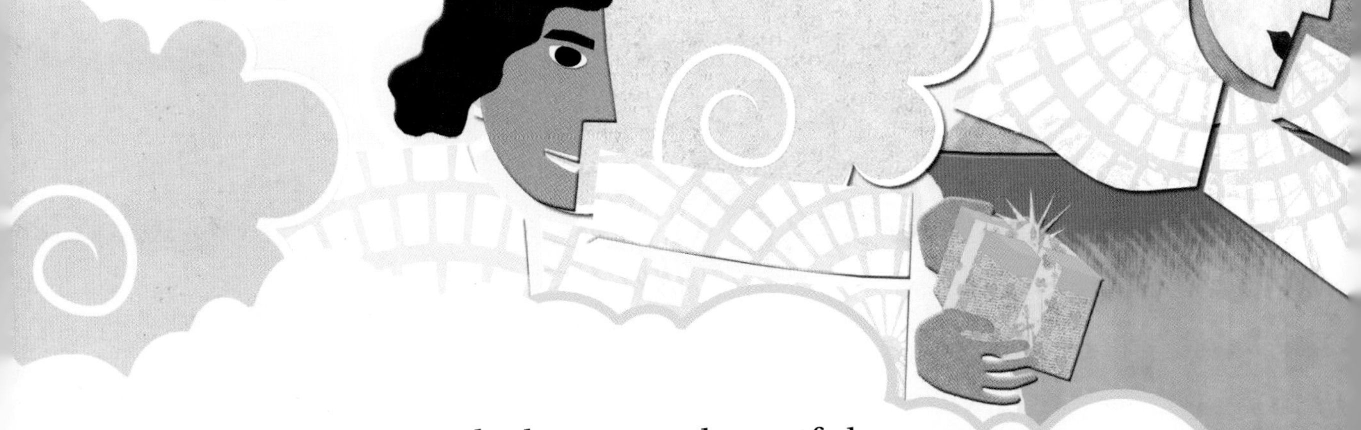

First, Zeus created the most beautiful woman. He then invited all of the gods to meet her. He told them to bring a gift. Being godly gifts, these gifts were very special. For example, Aphrodite gave the woman the gift of grace and charm. Apollo gave the woman the gift of musical talent.

"I will name the woman Pandora, which means 'all gifts,'" said Zeus.

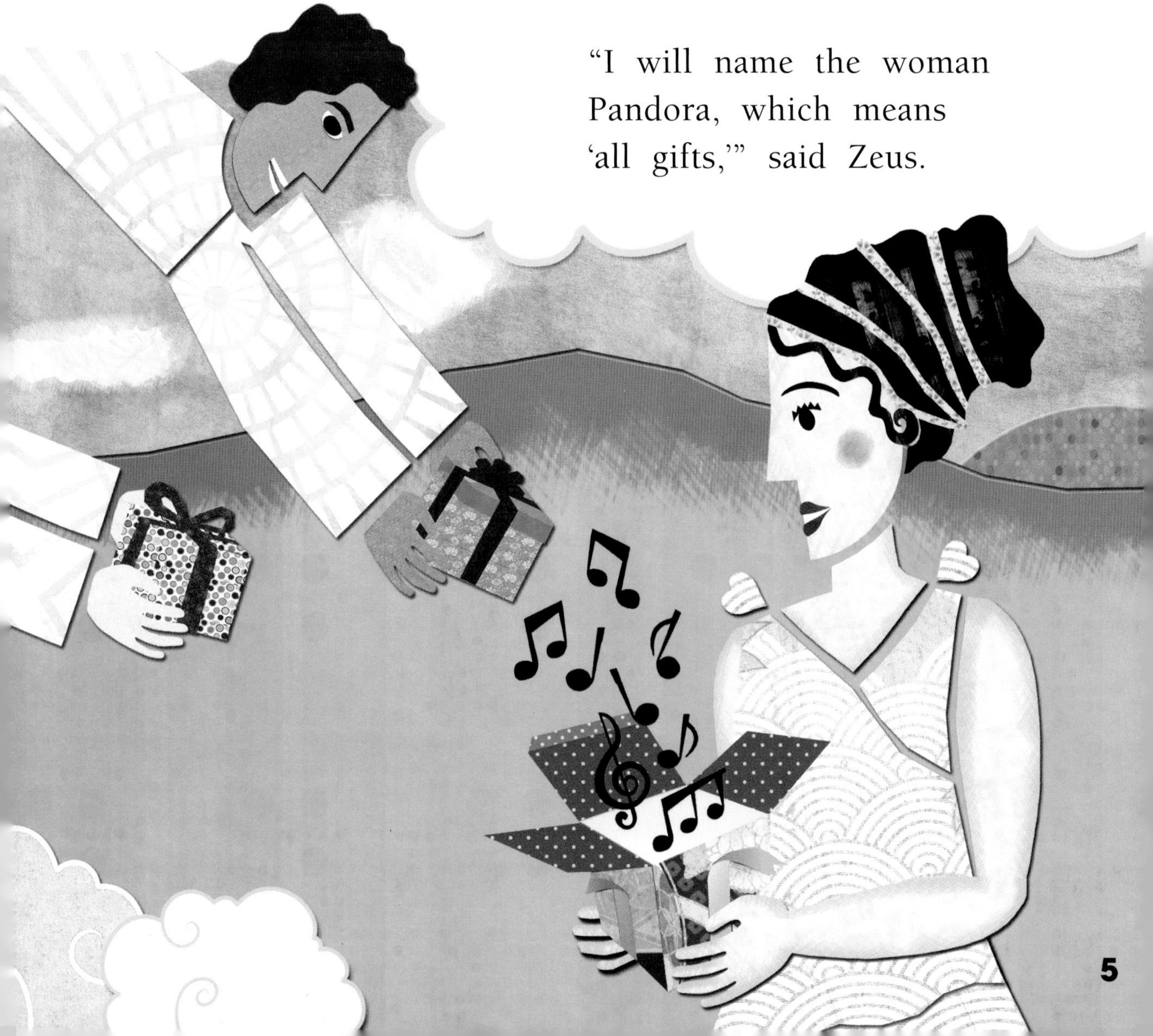

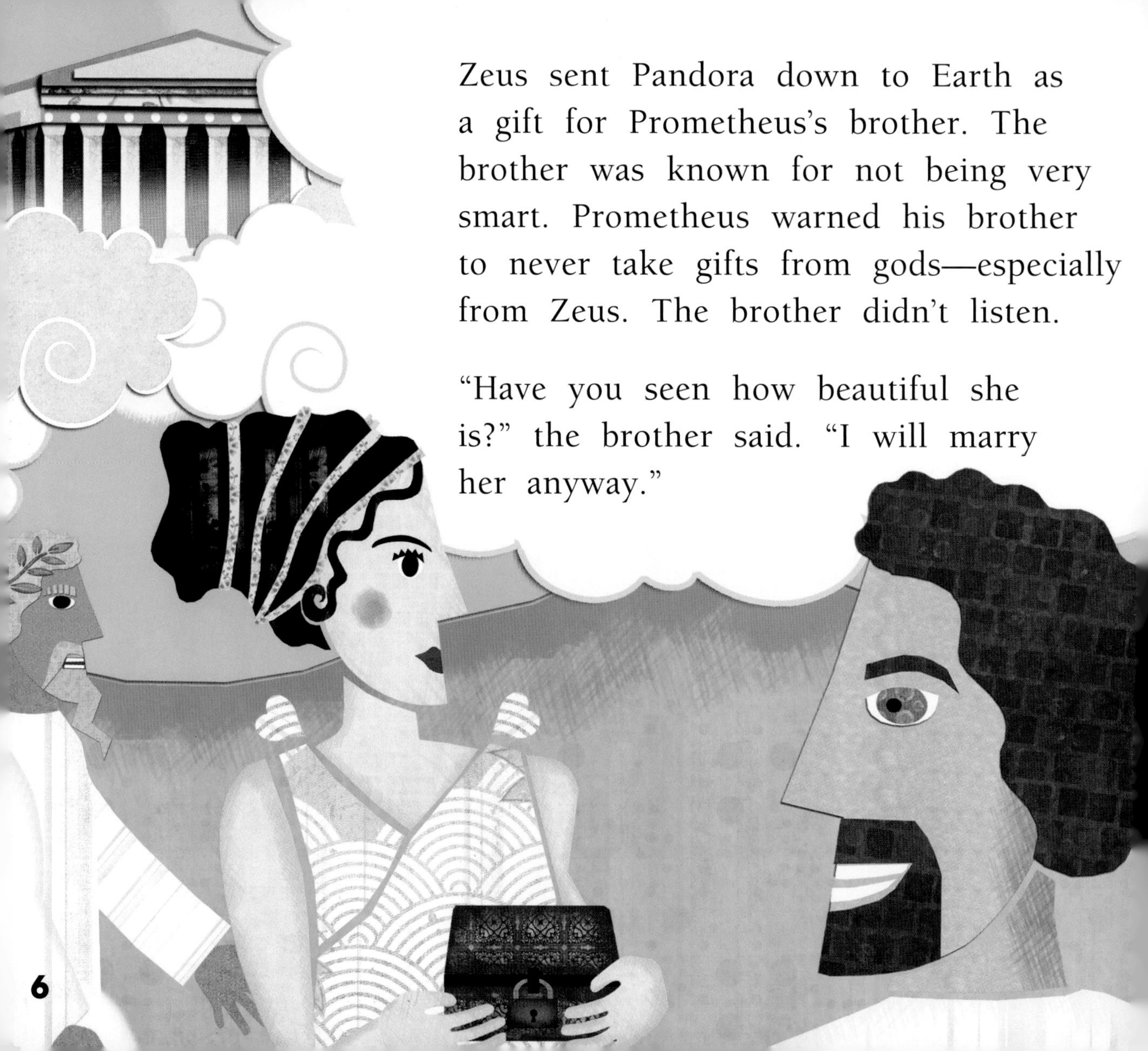

Zeus sent Pandora down to Earth as a gift for Prometheus's brother. The brother was known for not being very smart. Prometheus warned his brother to never take gifts from gods—especially from Zeus. The brother didn't listen.

"Have you seen how beautiful she is?" the brother said. "I will marry her anyway."

Pandora came to Earth holding a large box with a big lock on it. Zeus told her to give the box and the key to her husband.

"A warning to both of you," said Zeus. "Never, ever open this box!"

Along with beauty, charm, and talents, Pandora had also received the gift of curiosity. She was very curious about what might be in that box. What could be so precious that it needed a lock? She thought about the box day and night.

"Please, let's open it!" Pandora begged her husband. But he always said, "You know we cannot."

One day, as her husband was napping, Pandora stole the key!

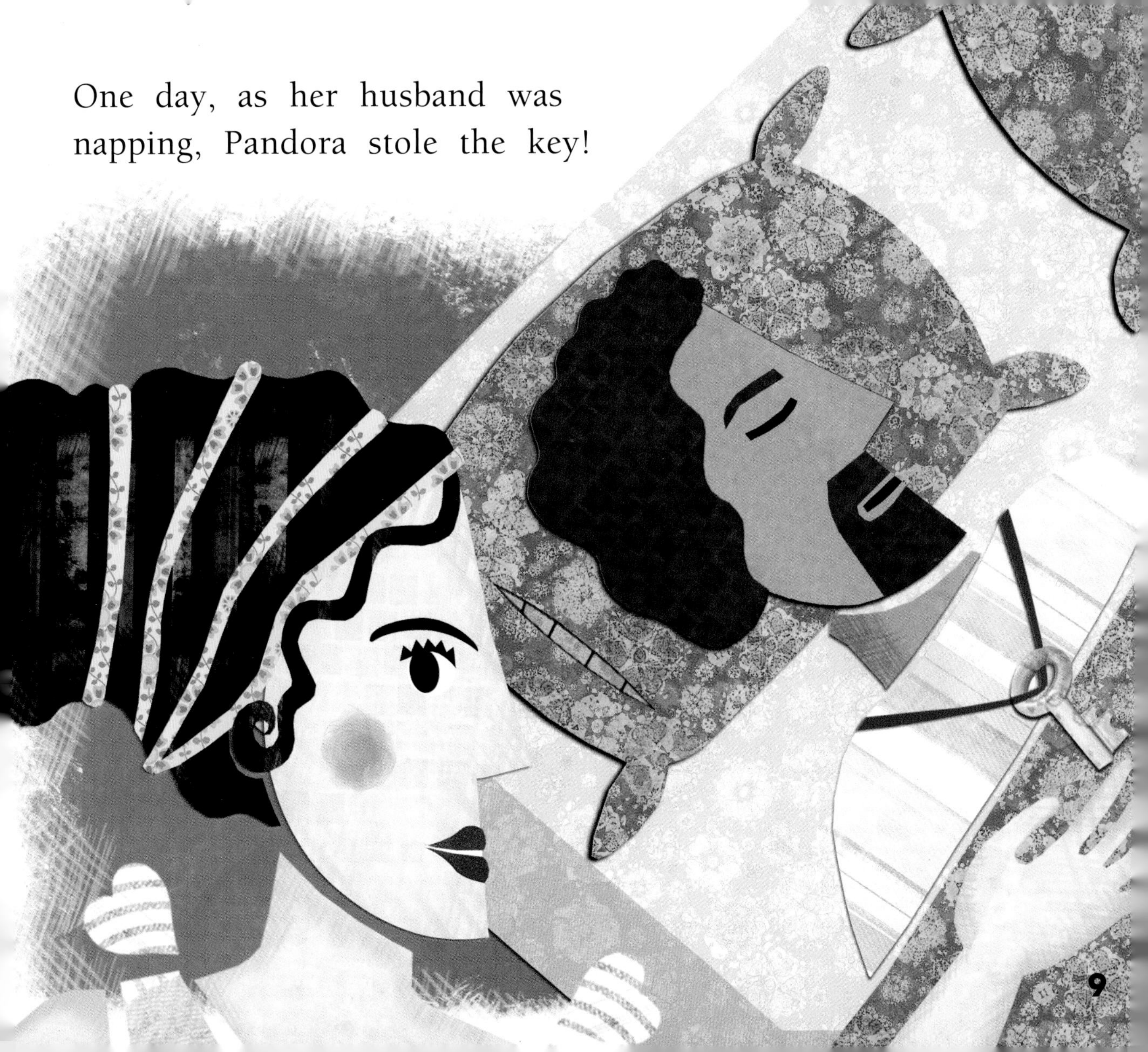

Pandora turned the key in the lock and slowly lifted the lid. In a burst of green smoke, out of the box flew every kind of ugly, horrible thing that humans fear.

Sickness! Worries!
Crime! Hate! Monsters!

Everything that bothered and haunted humans was released from the box. The bad things flew all over the place like angry bees, swarming and stinging.

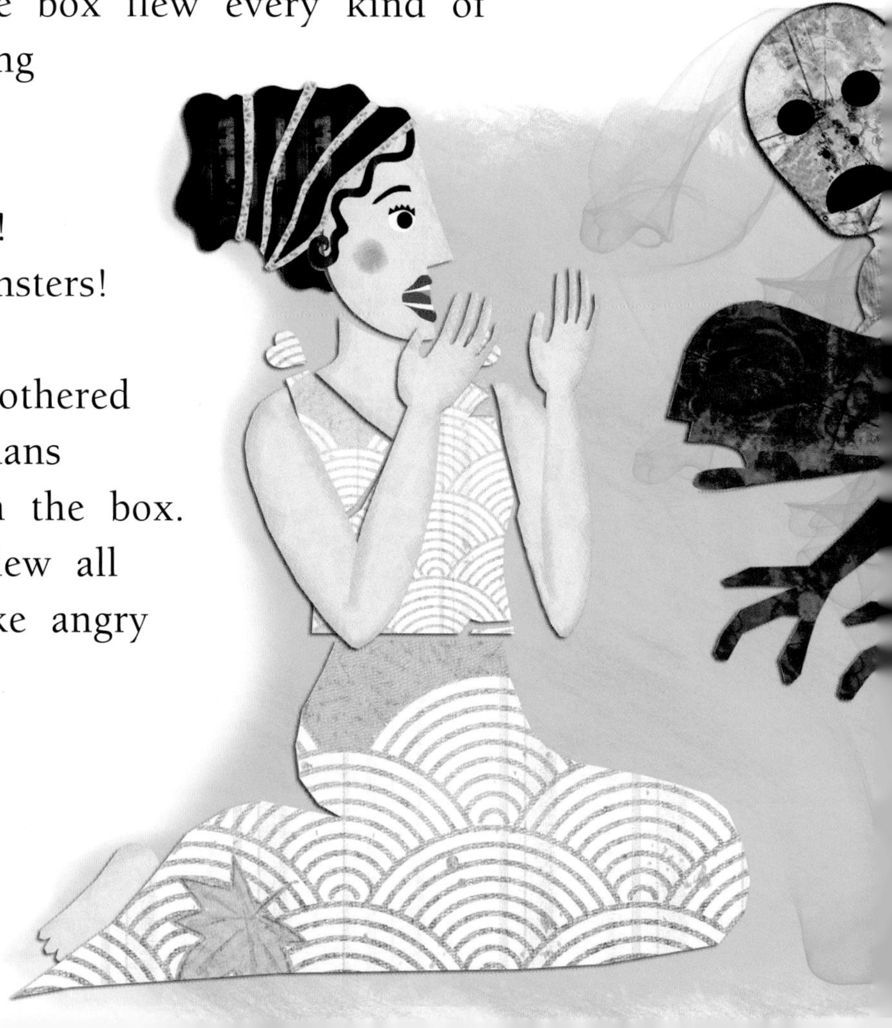

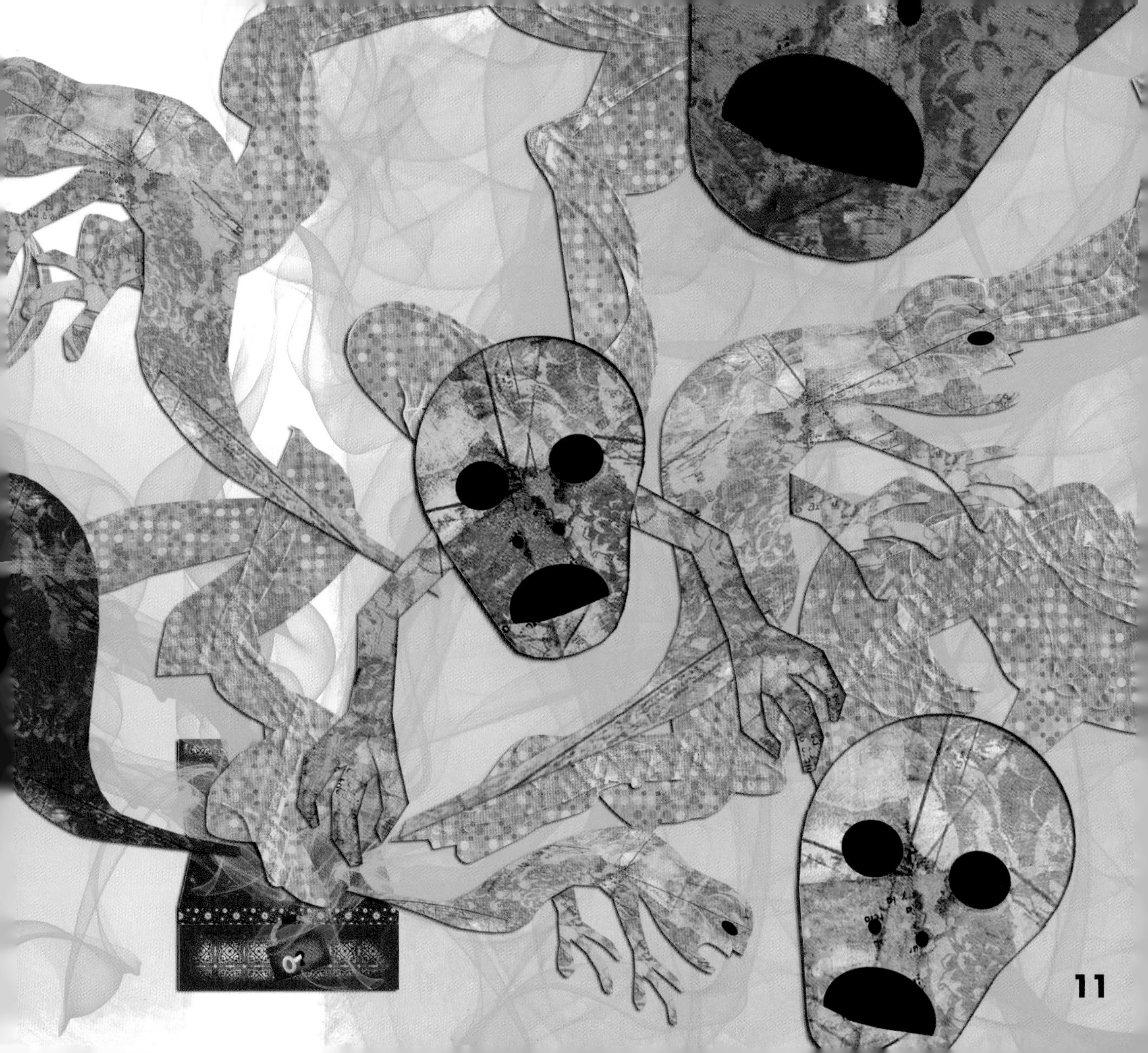

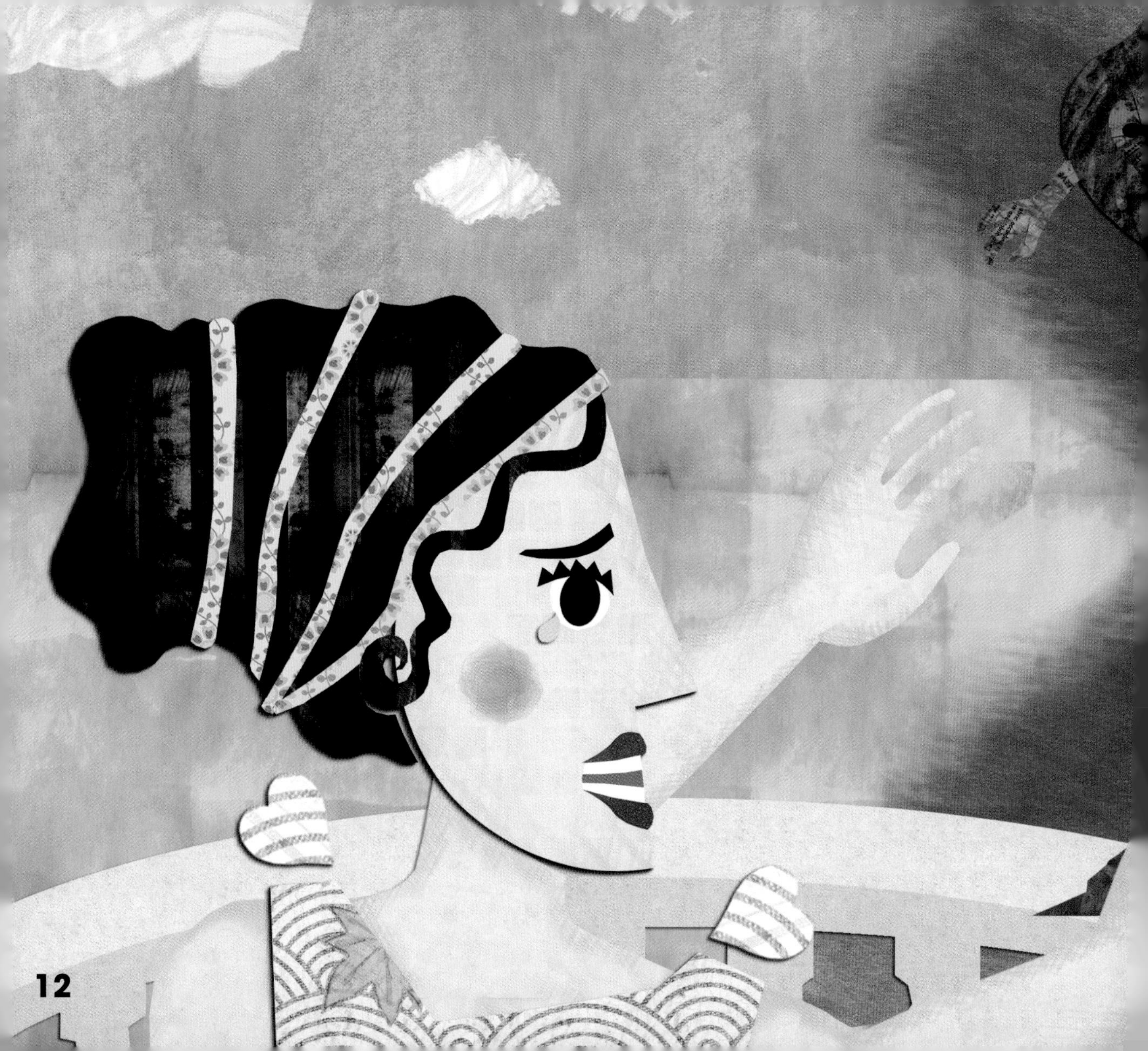

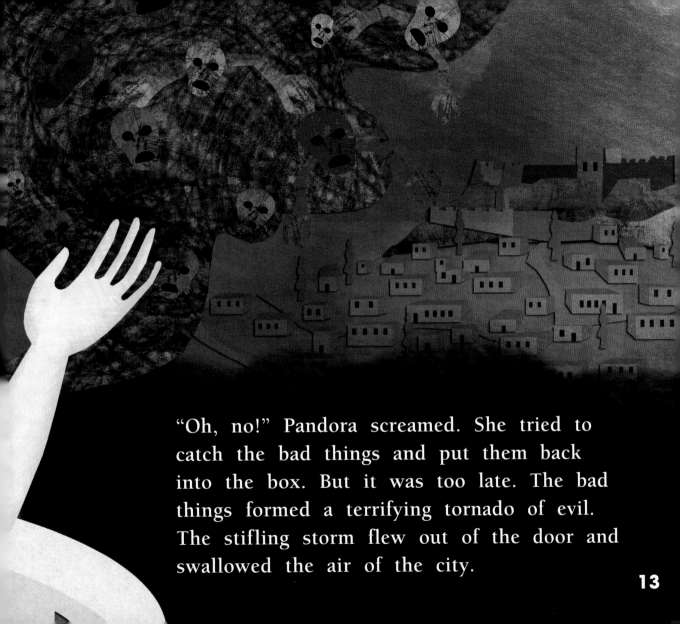

"Oh, no!" Pandora screamed. She tried to catch the bad things and put them back into the box. But it was too late. The bad things formed a terrifying tornado of evil. The stifling storm flew out of the door and swallowed the air of the city.

13

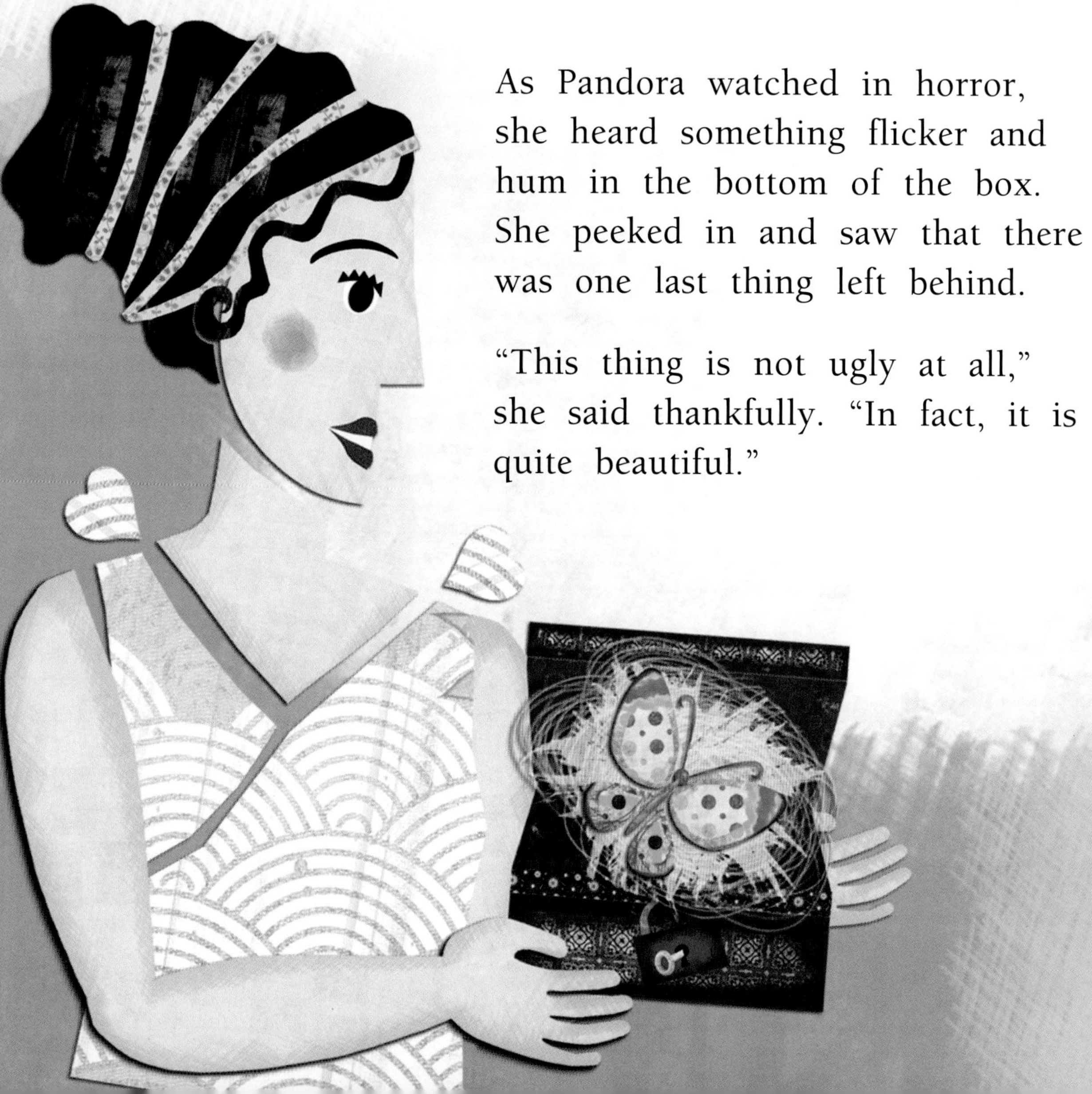

As Pandora watched in horror, she heard something flicker and hum in the bottom of the box. She peeked in and saw that there was one last thing left behind.

"This thing is not ugly at all," she said thankfully. "In fact, it is quite beautiful."

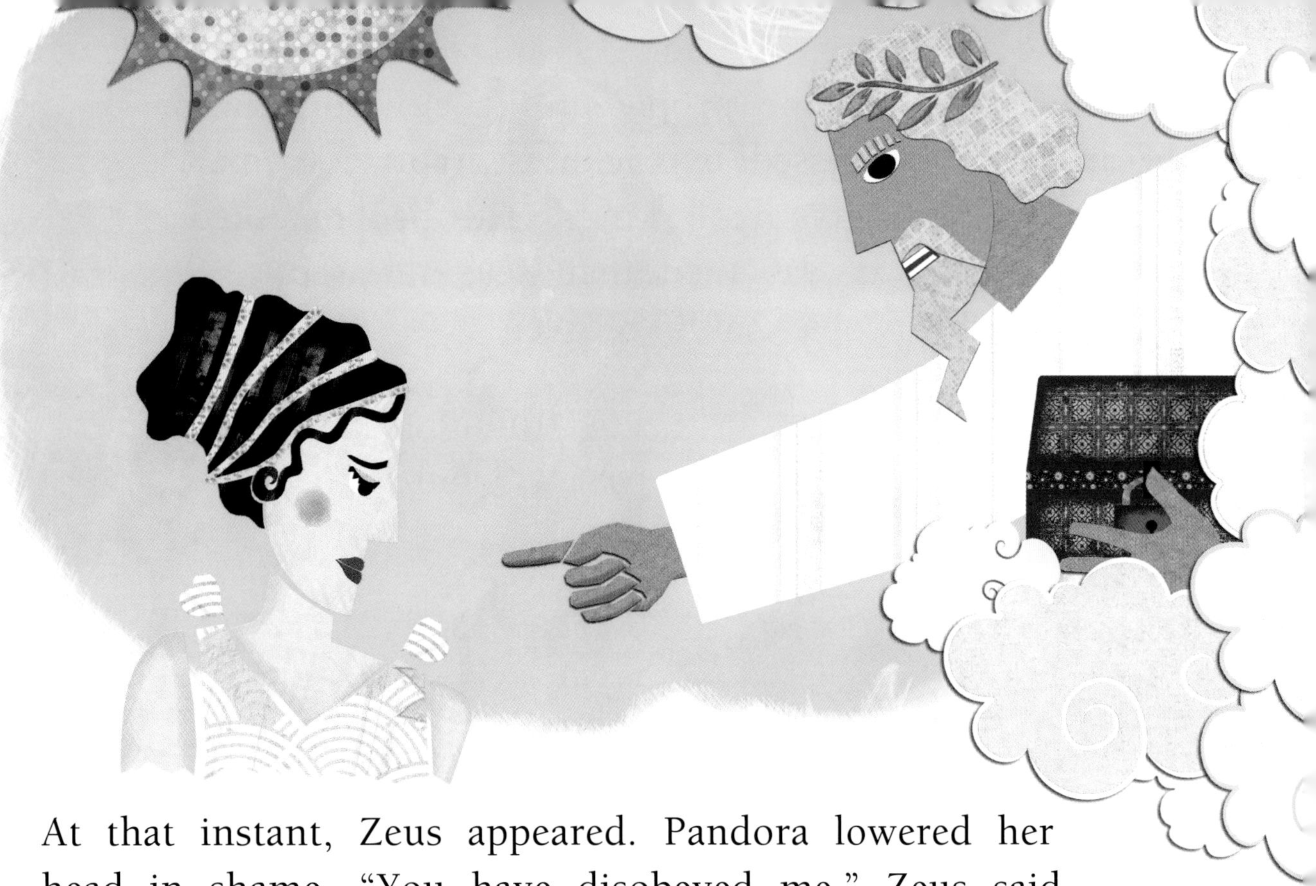

At that instant, Zeus appeared. Pandora lowered her head in shame. “You have disobeyed me,” Zeus said, pointing his finger at her. “Do you see this in the box? This is Hope. I will take back control of Hope.”

Zeus picked up the box and Hope, and went back up to Mount Olympus.

As time went on, the people of the city sometimes became very depressed by Sickness, Worry, Crime, Hate, and monsters of all kinds. The people asked Zeus for help. It was then that Zeus released Hope, so the people could recover.

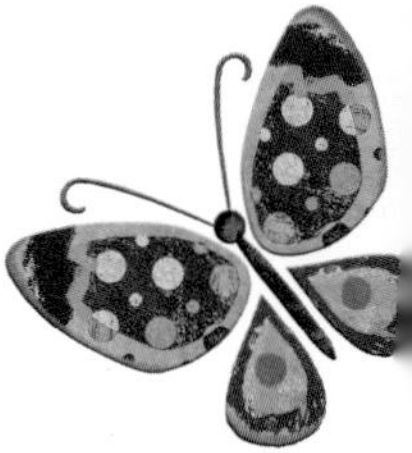

Even today, whatever evils are around us, we can receive Hope whenever we look for it.

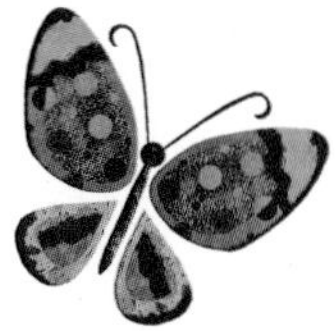

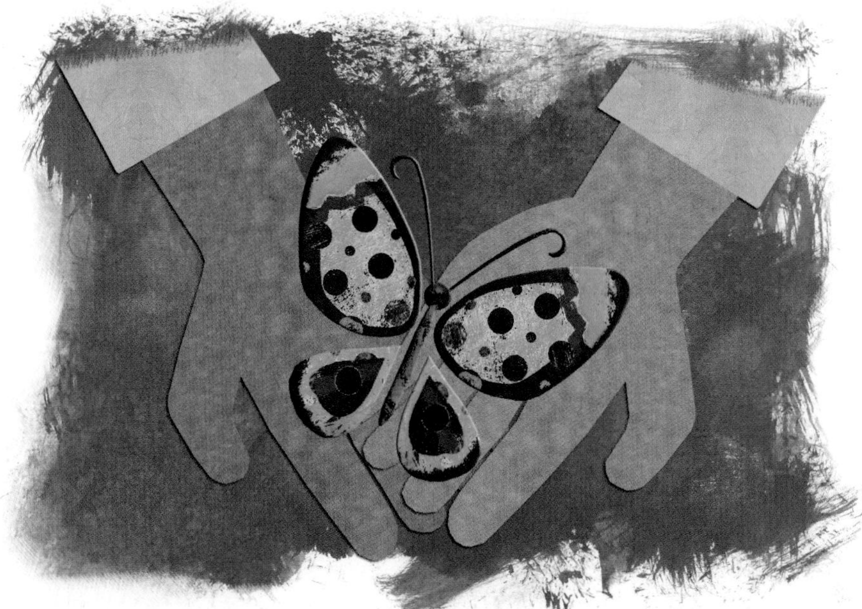